We looked far and wide to find the stars for our book. Then we realized that the perfect gang was right in our own kitchen—in the middle of the table.

Fruit—delicious, nutritious and perfumed by nature. What better cast for our wacky adventures?

This is a most unusual book, because you read it not only with your eyes, but also with your nose. If you go out and find our gang at the grocery store, then you can even experience this book with your sense of taste.

Each of our wonderful fragrances is introduced to you by different characters in our **WhiffyWear** plays. Take turns with your friends playing the different roles.

Good luck on the adventure.

Close your eyes and take a whiff…

MAC AND ANNIE APPLE

BILBO AND ANNA BANANA

SAM AND SALLY STRAWBERRY

ARACTERS

ALLIE AND OSCAR ORANGE

KIM AND COCO COCONUT

BETSY AND BILLY BUBBLEGUM

Apples are such a popular fruit
Their rosy red cheeks are so shiny and cute.
Here's Mac and Annie Apple
Hanging in their tree
Getting to know each other
And a bit of history.

ANNIE: Apple butter, Apple pie
       Where's the Apple of my eye?

MAC: (entering)
     Hi—I'm Mac Apple
     I'm green and I'm red.
     I'm like the Apple that fell
     On Sir Newton's head.

ANNIE: Oh! I'm Annie Apple,
       I live in this tree.
       But who was Sir Newton,
       explain it to me.

MAC: He was the man
Back in history
Who discovered the law
Of gravity.
It came to him suddenly
I've heard it said,
When one of my cousins
Fell on his head!

ANNIE: There were lots of other things
he discovered as well—
But if you scratch this patch,
You can soon tell
It was **WhiffyWear**
Who discovered our smell!

In warm breezy places where there's sun and there's sand,
Live lemons and grapefruits and the whole citrus clan.
Allie and Oscar are oranges you see,
The best smelling members of the whole family tree.

OSCAR: Hi Allie Orange, I sure love your hat!

ALLIE: I love yours too, but **wow**, what's that?

OSCAR: Its a portrait of our family tree.
        Uncle Grapefruit, Aunt Lemon, and **look**, there's me!

ALLIE: And there's Cousin Tangerine and the rest of us,
        Some big and some small, but all of us citrus.

OSCAR: We may have our differences, but still agree
        We love being loaded with vitamin C!

ALLIE: Vitamin C is really healthy I'm told,
You never will see an orange with a cold.

OSCAR: We're delicious, nutritious all of us kin,
And ever so juicy just under our skin!

ALLIE: We're like people in some ways
It can't be denied,
'Cause what's really important
Is deep down inside!

Sam and Sally Strawberry smiling in their sunny patch.
Strawberries, you ought to know, grow near the ground
Not on trees, that's not where they're found.
Leafy green with lovely, lively, luscious, yummy berries.
*STRAW*BERRIES, that is.

SAM: Don't you ever get tired being stuck on the ground?
        Don't you wish like a bird you could fly all around?

SALLY: I'd love to fly Sam, but not right this minute,
        That man's painting a picture, and I want to be in it.
        And if you wouldn't wiggle
        You could be in it yet,
          And we might get famous
          And hang in the Met!

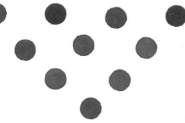

SAM: Oh Sal what a beautiful picture you'd make
Sitting on top of a big birthday cake.
You'd do well in a real big city,
After all, you're super pretty.

SALLY: A cake would be nice
But I've got a dream,
To swim in a bowl
Of fluffy whipped cream.

SAM: But we might get lonely so far from home,
We might start to miss the friends that we've known.

SALLY: But look Sam we have this picture to scratch,
To remember our sweet smelling strawberry patch!

Meet Anna Banana who lives in a bunch
Of these sweet smelling fruits, so good in your lunch.
And also we think you might like to know,
Her beautiful bunch-mate, Bilbo.

ANNA: Good evening Bilbo, how handsome you look,
Like you stepped from the pages of a high fashion book.

BILBO: And Anna my sweetheart, I do declare
I love that delicious perfume you wear.

ANNA: Bilbo it's true, the aroma is swell,
But it's no perfume, it's our own natural smell.

BILBO: Oh we bananas we're a radical fruit,
        Sweet smelling, delicious, nutritious . . .

ANNA: *AND CUTE!*

BILBO: Now sit for a moment and let me sing you a tune,
        My sweet Anna Banana shaped like the moon!

Chewy, white coconut, a famous fruit but.
It's also well known for being a nut.
Then why'd they call it coconut if it does so many things?
They should call them "Cow-co-fruity-sun-oil-nut-a-lings.

Kim and Coco Coconut live high up in a palm tree,
On a tropical island, near the warm blue sea.

COCO: You're a nut.

KIM: No, I'm a fruit.

COCO: Well one thing's for sure you're awful cu

KIM: But really, Coco—I'm confused.
I don't understand how.
I also have milk, am I a cow?

COCO: Well they call it milk and that's the truth,
But really it's more like a sweet tasting juice.

KIM: We're an odd combination, aren't we Co?

COCO: Yes, cause there's more about us you really should know
They use our oils for their lotions,
Our trees for their shade,
And from our leaves mats and baskets are made.

KIM: Oh Coco I really never did see
All the wonderful delicious things we could be.
We'll never get bored, or stuck in a rut.

COCO: But Kimmy, to me, you're still a nut.

Bubblegum Bubblegum, delicious to taste,
Bubblegum Bubblegum, sticky as paste,
Bubblegum Bubblegum is good in its place,
But a bubble is trouble
When it pops in your face!

BETSY: I wonder what a couple of Bubblegums like
us are doing in a book like this? This book is
all about a nut and some fruits!

BILLY: Have you ever heard of a
Bubblegum Tree?

BETSY: Boy that sounds pretty crazy to me!

BILLY: Well, just like apples and oranges
and coconuts you see,
The gum for our bubbles does
come from a tree.

BETSY: But what kind of a tree?

BILLY: A Gum Tree you know.

BETSY: But where does it grow?

BILLY: In South America
and Mexico.

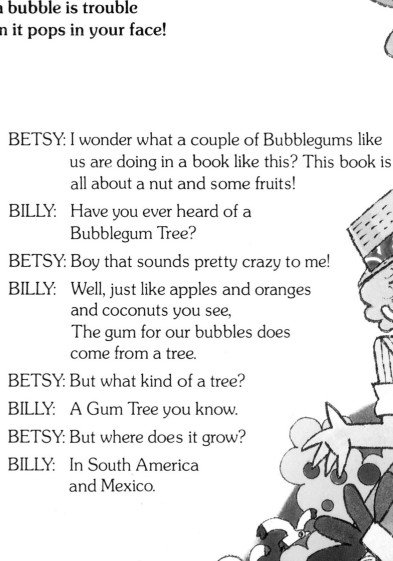

BETSY: *THEN* what do they do with us? Ship us up here?

BILLY: Yes, then they mix us and fix us and wrap us, my dear.

BETSY: So we're sorta like oranges, apples and fruit.
       We're juicy, delicious and smell good to boot.
       So scratch us,
       And sniff us
       And you'll understand why,
       We're in this book
       With these other guys.

CLAUDINE'S DREAM

I dreamed I saw a rainbow sky
With a river of colors flowing by.
The children of the world were gathered there,
With fruits and flowers everywhere.

And even in my dream I dreamed
I hitched a ride on a star that gleamed
To a giant tree with magic blooms
That filled the air with sweet perfumes.

And from the center of this tree
Came the song of a small white bird,
Bringing peace and unity
To everyone who heard.

That peaceful song is with me yet
I know I never will forget.
And I want the world to be
The way it was beneath that tree.